Canada Day

Heather Kissock

Georges Vanier Elementary
6985-142 St., Surrey, BC V3W 5N1
LIBRARY

Weigl

Published by Weigl Educational Publishers Limited
6325 10 Street S.E.
Calgary, Alberta
T2H 2Z9

www.weigl.com
Copyright ©2010 WEIGL EDUCATIONAL PUBLISHERS LIMITED
All rights reserved. No part of this publication may be reproduced, stored in a retrieval system, or transmitted in any form or by any means, electronic, mechanical, photocopying, recording, or otherwise, without the prior written permission of the publisher.

Library and Archives Canada Cataloguing in Publication data available upon request.
Fax 403-233-7769 for the attention of the Publishing Records department.

ISBN 978-1-55388-520-7 (hard cover)
ISBN 978-1-55388-525-2 (soft cover)

Printed in the United States of America
1 2 3 4 5 6 7 8 9 0 13 12 11 10 09

Editor: Heather C. Hudak
Design: Terry Paulhus

Every reasonable effort has been made to trace ownership and to obtain permission to reprint copyright material. The publishers would be pleased to have any errors or omissions brought to their attention so that they may be corrected in subsequent printings.

Weigl acknowledges Getty Images as its primary image supplier for this title.
Alamy: page 13; Toronto Public Library: page 9.

We gratefully acknowledge the financial support of the Government of Canada through the Book Publishing Industry Development Program (BPIDP) for our publishing activities.

Contents

What is Canada Day? 4
Being Canadian 6
Creating Canada 8
Confederation 10
Dominion Day 12
A New Constitution........................14
Picnics, Parties, and Parades..........16
Canada's Special Song 18
Symbols of Canada 20
Becoming Canadian 22
Glossary/Index.............................. 24

What is Canada Day?

July 1 is Canada Day. This is when Canadians celebrate the **joining** together of the provinces and territories as one country. It is a time when people think about what it means to be Canadian.

Being Canadian

When people think about Canada, they might think of a large nation that stretches from the Pacific to the Arctic to the Atlantic Oceans. There are many parks and green spaces for people to enjoy. People also may think about how many Canadians are friendly and **peace**-loving. People of all cultures are free to celebrate their traditions.

Creating Canada

Canada was created on July 1, 1867. This is when four provinces agreed to join together to become a country. These provinces were Nova Scotia, New Brunswick, Quebec, and Ontario. Before this time, Canada was ruled by Great Britain.

Confederation

The joining of these provinces was called Confederation. The new country was known as the Dominion of Canada. By 1905, 11 provinces and territories had joined Confederation. In 1949, Newfoundland and Labrador was the last province to join. The territory of Nunavut was formed in 1999.

Dominion Day

The Dominion of Canada had a big party for its first birthday. Birthday celebrations took place in the following years as well. These events were called Dominion Day.

A New Constitution

The Dominion of Canada signed a new Constitution in 1982. The country was no longer under British rule. Its name was changed to Canada. The holiday celebrated on July 1 then became known as Canada Day.

Picnics, Parties, and Parades

Many people do not have to work or go to school on Canada Day. They have picnics, parties, and parades. There often are fireworks at night.

Canada's Special Song

Some people sing *O Canada* on Canada Day. This is the country's national **anthem**. The song was written in French in 1880. It has since been written in English as well.

O Canada (1880)

O Canada!
Terre de nos aïeux,
Ton front est ceint
de fleurons glorieux!

Car ton bras sait porter l'épée,
Il sait porter la croix!

Ton histoire est une épopée
Des plus brillants exploits.

Et ta valeur, de foi trempée,
Protégera nos foyers et nos droits.

Protégera nos foyers et nos droits.

O Canada (1980)

O Canada!
Our home and native land!
True patriot love in all thy
sons command.

With glowing hearts we see thee rise,
The True North strong and free!

From far and wide,
O Canada, we stand on
guard for thee.

God keep our land glorious and free!
O Canada, we stand on guard
for thee.

O Canada, we stand on
guard for thee.

Symbols of Canada

The maple leaf is a symbol of Canada. Some people paint maple leaves on their body on Canada Day. Other people carry the Canadian flag. It has a maple leaf at its centre. The flag is red and white. These colours are also symbols of Canada.

Becoming Canadian

People sometimes move to Canada from other countries. Many of these people choose to become Canadian **citizens** on Canada Day. It is a special day for these new Canadians and all people who live in Canada.

Glossary

Index

celebration 4, 6, 12, 14

Confederation 10

July 1 4, 8, 14

maple leaf 20

O Canada 18, 19

provinces 4, 8, 10